RANCHO CUCAMONGA
PUBLIC LIBRARY

D0647054

SIR REGINALD'S LOGBOOK

Text and illustrations © 2008 Matt Hammill

All rights reserved. No part of this publication may be reproduced, stored in a retrieval system or transmitted, in any form or by any means, without the prior written permission of Kids Can Press Ltd. or, in case of photocopying or other reprographic copying, a license from The Canadian Copyright Licensing Agency (Access Copyright). For an Access Copyright license, visit www.accesscopyright.ca or call toll free to 1-800-893-5777.

Kids Can Press acknowledges the financial support of the Government of Ontario, through the Ontario Media Development Corporation's Ontario Book Initiative; the Ontario Arts Council; the Canada Council for the Arts; and the Government of Canada, through the BPIDP, for our publishing activity.

Published in Canada by
Kids Can Press Ltd.
29 Birch Avenue
Toronto, ON M4V 1E2

Published in the U.S. by
Kids Can Press Ltd.
2250 Military Road
Tonawanda, NY 14150

www.kidscanpress.com

The art in this book was rendered in ink, watercolor and pastel.
The text is set in McKracken.

Edited by Tara Walker   Designed by Karen Powers
Printed and bound in Singapore

This book is smyth sewn casebound.

CM 08 0 9 8 7 6 5 4 3 2 1

Library and Archives Canada Cataloguing in Publication

Hammill, Matt
    Sir Reginald's logbook / Matt Hammill.
ISBN 978-1-55453-202-5
I. Title.
PS8615.A542S57 2008   jC813'.6   C2007-906556-2

Kids Can Press is a [orus™ Entertainment company

For Mom and Dad

SIR REGINALD'S LOGBOOK

by Matt Hammill

KIDS CAN PRESS

RANCHO CUCAMONGA
PUBLIC LIBRARY

AUGUST 16TH, 9:21 P.M.

I begin this journal by the flickering glow of my campfire. Although it is late, I'm far too excited for sleep as tomorrow marks the beginning of my greatest quest! What perils and pitfalls await my search for the legendary Lost Tablet of Illusion? I shudder to imagine. Should I not survive, I only hope this record has a chance to outlive me.

And why should I, Sir Reginald,
fear for my safety? Well ...

... the jungle is a dangerous place.

AUGUST 17TH, 8:09 A.M.

I awoke with a start this morning, and I could
have sworn the sound that summoned me
from my slumber was the deafening buzz
of the Carnivorous Elephant Beetle!

BUZZ BUZZ BUZZ

However, once I'd scrambled to my feet, there was no sign of it — only the faint echo of its call.

But I must begin the day's journey, for according to my calculations, the Lost Tablet of Illusion lies not far from here. I assemble my equipment:

buzz buzz buzz buzz buzz

One safari hat

One instrument of defence

One logbook (this one!) and lucky pen

One pair of hiking boots

And one uncommonly clever and resourceful mind!

With everything in order, I depart.

As I approach the resting place of the Lost Tablet, I review its legendary properties in my mind. It's said that this artifact gives its possessor the power to cast captivating spells of illusion. Can such a device even exist? I shall soon find out!

8:52 A.M.

AHA! That pedestal yonder — if memory serves me, that's where the Lost Tablet of Illusion lies. It's almost within my grasp!

8:55 A.M.

GADZOOKS!

The Tablet — it's gone! STOLEN!

And what's this? Footprints?
What manner of beast has robbed
my heart of its most fervent desire?
This offence shall not go unpunished!
I begin pursuit at once!

But, oh, the monstrous
size of these tracks!

AND SUCH
HUGE
CLAWS!

I must be cautious.

9:17 A.M.

The footprints led me to the yawning mouth of a vast cave, and I ventured boldly inside. Although I found no traces of the Tablet, I was afforded the chance to study a colony of Gargantuan Vampire Bats in their natural habitat ...

... which turned out to be a
most unfortunate opportunity.

One of them was
particularly aggressive.

But I wrestled it to
the ground ...

... and made sure that the last blood
that monster ever tasted was its own.
But enough time has been wasted
here — somewhere ahead,
the Tablet awaits!

9:40 A.M.

WHAT A FRIGHT! I was just now stopped dead in my tracks as I beheld, stretched across my path, the sinuous form of the lethal Tiger-Stripe Viper!

But upon closer inspection, I realized I had made a misidentification. What I'd thought was the vicious Viper was in reality merely its shed skin. It was quite hollow.

I checked.

10:07 A.M.
And so I must continue the hunt. But these footprints ... they trouble me. I'm normally quite skilled in the identification of animal species, yet this creature eludes me. No matter! I shall come upon it soon enough.

That glimmer of blue I see up ahead — could that be water?

10:25 A.M.

Water it was — a dark, murky lake.
However, when I tried to skirt its quiet surface,
something cold and wet seized my ankle
and I was blinded by a brilliant light!
My heart leapt into my throat as I recognized,
towering before me, the glowing lure of
the Great Purple Angler-Fish!

But in the next moment, the light had vanished and the lake was still once more. The fiend had returned to its depths and, miraculously, I had been spared.

I left quickly.

The hunt continues ...

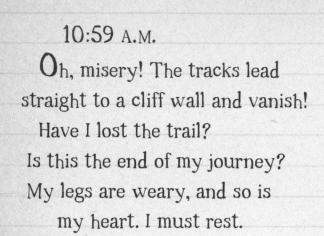

10:59 A.M.
Oh, misery! The tracks lead straight to a cliff wall and vanish! Have I lost the trail? Is this the end of my journey? My legs are weary, and so is my heart. I must rest.

TAP TAP TAP

11:16 A.M.
Astonishingly, there seems to
be a sound coming from within
the rock. Could there be more to
this wall than I perceive?
I must investigate!

11:20 A.M.

Remarkable! There was indeed another side to that cliff — and a passageway through! But even more marvelous than the passage itself was the rare specimen that awaited me on the other side: a full-grown Bright-Eyed Baboon!

No sooner had the brute detected my presence than it charged at me with one skinny hand outstretched. I jumped to the ready. But the monkey must have realized it was outmatched, for it froze and then backed away awkwardly.

I'll never forget the almost-human twinkle of intelligence in its dark eyes.

11:28 A.M.

Now that the baboon has fled, I'm able to take note of my surroundings on the other side of the wall. The air here is different — cooler. And do I detect sunlight peeking through the trees above? But more importantly, I'm back on the creature's trail!

11:31 A.M.

Oh my! These tracks are fresh!

11:44 A.M.

My hand trembles as I write this,
but unless my eyes deceive me, I,
Sir Reginald, have located my quarry!
And what a beast it is! It stalks the
foot of a ruined temple, and even
from here I can feel the earth
quake with each step.

And there, among the littered bones
— the LOST TABLET OF ILLUSION!
Dare I approach?
Dare I risk being devoured alive
for the sake of my quest?

OF COURSE I DO!

My foe put forth a
ferocious effort ...

But I discovered its weakness!

11:56 A.M.

I'VE DONE IT! I, Sir Reginald, have recovered the Lost Tablet of Illusion! I sit now atop the temple. The beast below seems much smaller from this height.

Perhaps I'll name this species the Fire-Eyed Double-Fang, or "Fido" for short!

And now I must return to my encampment to see if the Tablet retains its legendary magic ...

12:00 NOON

It does! Now at last, with the
Tablet in hand, I may finally relax.
It's been a long morning, indeed.

And, oh, the power of
these illusions!

So captivating, so —
   But wait. What's this?

It appears a
new adventure is afoot!